Tied

a one-man play

by Crystal Rae

© 2018

Library of Congress Cataloging-in-Publication Data

 Rae, Crystal. Tied, a one man play/ Crystal Rae ISBN-978-0-57864-785-2

Headshot Photo by Justin Taplet Cover Design by ViknCharlie - Fiverr.com

Acknowledgments

This work is in honor of my father, my brother, my nephew, uncles and the handful of men who have stood as pillars, guide posts, and umbrellas in my life. To the women of my life, my mother, grandmother, sister, niece, and aunts, and cousins galore, I hope to make you proud. Thank you to The Ensemble Theatre of Houston, Texas who has made room for my ideas in the way a mother hen makes room for her chicks. I am grateful.

Thanks to the enormous talent that is Jason Carmichael and his willingness to perform draft after draft. You sir, was God choosing to show off. I am grateful to every person who sat through readings, lent advice, and read copies of the play. Thanks to City Life Church, you are a pivotal part of my tale and that cannot be understated. Thank you my tribe of friends who have the arduous task of reading everything always, until I die, you're awesome.

Character: Daniel - Age 35-65, African-American.

Time: 1964

Setting: The front porch of Daniel's mind, Alabama. In a Negro neighborhood on a street that's one notch above modest and headed on the road toward middle class.

ACT 1

Sc.1

DANIEL

My mother named us Moses, Joshua,
Elijah, and Daniel — in that
order — and folks would see my
brothers, especially if they
meeting us for the first time,
and without fail, we could count
on somebody saying: (he sings)
"Go Down Moses." And Joshua had
"Joshua fit the Battle of
Jericho," and Elijah had "Elijah
Rock," but they'd get to me and
there wasn't no music for me.
When you small, stuff like that
seep into places it wouldn't if
you was older. Seem like you got
more cracks in you when you
small, like a soft spot on your

4

head... except your whole heart's
like that. Now they wouldn't sing
to me, but what they would say is
"Oh, I should tell you my dream!"

So, I adapted. Set me up a small
business. Kids would bring me
they candy money and tell me
their dreams and I was making a
killing coming up with all kinds
of stuff. About four months in
and I had $234.45 in nickels,
dimes, and pennies. Which wasn't
nothing to sneeze at, not in them
days. My momma gave me the
soundest beating of my whole life
when she found out. When my daddy
came home, he got an earful from
her. And then he called me into
that kitchen. Which in my house,
operated like a court room
whenever we was in trouble. Until
then, I didn't know my top lip
could sweat. My whole top lip was
a swimming pool, my nose was
sweating, my eyes was sweating.
Looked like I'd been baptized
fully dressed.

I showed him everything. The journal with the names, the dreams kids had, my "interpretations," the money I'd charged. I'd kept a record of all of it. There were repeat customers who said my interpretations were dead on, and I pretended like it was The Spirit, but some people was just easy to make out. I was 8 years old keeping my own books cause it made sense. Seem like I should know what I had told folks, in case they needed a reminder or a refund. My daddy thumbed through every page. Sent my mother out the room. And kneeled on the floor so he and I was right here.

(He motions eye to
eye.)

He says to me, "I was there when you was being born. Right there in the next room, like I was for the other three, listening, pacing,

probably the only time I ever
prayed about something other than
dinner was when y'all was being
born. Yo' momma sounded like she
was being killed each time. And
after a few hours of your momma
screaming, Ol' Sista' Winston
she'd say, "Oh! We got ourselves a
boy." And I was listening for that
when you was coming. And she ain't
say that. She said "Oh" and I
stopped walking when I heard that
"oh." And I hear, "We got
ourselves a problem." I wasn't
supposed to come in, women folk
got all kinda wives' tales about
it, but I wasn't trying hear
through no door what the problem
was. Wasn't gonna be no problems
and I not see about 'em. Not in my
house. I come in there and the
women scream like chickens in a
coop, and your momma look like she
was seeing a ghost but she
breathing. And Ol' Winston is
stooped over something wiggling
and writhing and I see it's you,
looking like a purple grape. You

had the cord wrapped 'round your
neck seem like thirty times, and
she's yanking at it like a ball of
yarn, trying to get you untangled.
And then your wiggling stopped.
And Sista' Winston hands went to
shaking and my eyes was going from
her, to you, to her, to you and I
threw that 87 year old woman
against the dresser, just threw
her. I apologized later, and I
scooped you up and yanked off the
rest of that chord. And I said to
whoever was listening, I said: "If
his own spirit won't stay here,
give him mine. Give him everything
I ain't using, give him everything
I got, he can have it all right
now." I had you right here, you
was staining up my good shirt, and
you was warm, but so still. And I
pulled you back to look at you and
your eyes were open. And I
hollered right in your face — I
don't know if I was trying to show
you what you was supposed to be
doing, or what, but I held you to
my face, as close as you is now,

8

and I roared, and then your eyes
got this big a round and you
roared back and...and arched and
screamed. And I roared again, and
you roared, and we was hollering
for at least an hour." When I tell
you, that is the only time I have
ever seen my dad cry. That was the
only time I ever see my daddy cry!
Not break down, he ain't break
down, but there was tears from
nowhere. I think it surprised him,
I mean he wiped his face so quick
looking confused, like he wasn't
sure what was happening to him.
And I grabbed him. Wrapped my ashy
arms around his neck and it was a
lifetime before he put his arm
around me. But he did, and he
says, "Proud of you."

(Daniel stands up)

And then he got up. Made himself
a drink and walked out the
kitchen. Momma made me give back
every single dime. Which wasn't

hard, I hadn't spent a cent. She
asked me if I'd learned my lesson
and I said I had. But I ain't
tell her what I learned cause I
didn't want me another beating. I
learned, it ain't just my spirit
walking around in here (points to
his chest). I got my father
trapped inside. And maybe his
father, and his father's father,
ain't no telling. But I got they
rage in my chest, they fire, they
hope, all of that is mixed in
with mine, and there ain't no
changing it. And there ain't no
wanting to.

Sc.2

The real Daniel had visions and
dreams and such all the time. Not
me. When I'm awake, I'm awake,
and when I'm sleep, it's black. I
don't see nothing, don't hear
nothing till it's time to get up.
Been that way my whole life. Then
1963 hits and I'm dreaming.

Color, sounds, all of it, and
it's clear as you standing there.
In the dream I'm standing in a
street, somewhere downtown, folks
walking by, cars honking. It's
the middle of the day, ain't no
reason for me to be there right
in the middle of the street. But
I'm looking up at the sky and got
my arms spread out like you do
when the lands been in a drought
for months, and suddenly rain
drops fall. Cars whizzing by and
I got my arms open and my head
all the way back, laughing. And
my tie starts feeling tight, so I
go to let it down a bit. The
tie's got scales on it. The point
of the tie at the bottom turn up
and look at me. It's a snake, but
it ain't a snake, and it's
tightening around my neck, and
I'm clawing at it, and my knees
buckle, and I can't get it off.
And somebody on the curb is
singing, while I'm being
strangled to death, not helping
mind you, just singing.

(DANIEL sings Negro
spiritual, "Oh
Freedom".)

Before I'll be a slave
I'll be buried in my
grave. I'll be buried in
my grave. I'll be buried
in my grave!

Sc.3

First night I woke myself up cause
I had thrown myself out the bed
fighting a navy blue necktie. My
wife say, "That's cause you ate
Sista' Greer's cake and didn't
have none of mine." A jealous
women is the worst kind. Took her
two weeks to even ask me what the
dream was about. And when she
heard it, she didn't like it.
"Snakes ain't never no good sign,"
she say. Like I ain't know snakes

ain't never no good sign. One
morning, I woke up to find I had
scratched my whole neck up, and
busted my own lip, and my baby
girl, the youngest one, she says,
"Daddy, you had that dream again?"
and I say, "Yeah baby," and she
say, "My teacher got a book
called, Other Lands. It's full of
pictures of people from all over
like China, and South America and
I looked at all the pictures of
the folks from Africa, and didn't
none of them have no neckties on.
Even the chiefs, they wasn't
wearing 'em. Maybe where we come
from — they ain't got no
neckties." And I heard that and it
was like all the mysteries of the
world got solved. It ain't ours.
That ain't what she said, but
that's what she was meaning.

These words I'm talking right
now, coming out my mouth right
now, they ain't ours, these
trousers, suspenders, neckties,
none of it. We adapt. We try and

fit in, try to do it like you ask
us. We say "Yes Sir" "No Sir",
move off the sidewalk, sit in the
back, wait on justice to try our
cases, we bide our time and hold
our tongues, and wait our turn,
and do it all like you tell us
and ain't none of that way ours!
None of it. It wasn't just some
light that went off in my head.
It was the sun rising. Maybe
where we come from, they don't
wear neckties.

Whoever in here. Whoever locked
inside my chest, he remember why
we clap on 2 and 4. He say, there
is power in the Earth and you
stomp and let the power shoot
through your whole body and
explode out your hands. Someone
in here know if I'm supposed to
be wearing tiger's teeth on a
necklace, or warrior paint under
my eyes, or tattoos on my chest.
Ain't all of me forgot. Someone
in me know the truth and he won't
wear the tie. He see it for what

it is and he been fighting for me
to remember. After all that
revelation, I did the only thing
I could do for my daughter. I
picked her up, spun her around,
and she was laughing, and I was
laughing, and I stopped with her
still in the air. And for the
first time in 38 years, I roared.
I felt it coming up the way you
feel a sob coming, felt like my
whole soul wanted to tear through
my skin. It was my daddy roaring,
and my grandfather, and his
father — they was all screaming
in my head at the same time and
it was coming out my throat. All
of us, roaring. And I tell you,
her eyes got this big around —
and she roared back. And I roared
and she roared again; and we was
like that 'til my arms starting
burning cause she ain't as small
as she used to be; and we marched
right into my bedroom, tore open
the little closet I had, and she
helped me throw them neckties in
the trash — every single one.

When we was finished, the room
felt clean. Ain't that something?
That was Friday, September 13th,
19 and 63. And on Sunday she was
gone.

> (DANIEL rocks gently, is off
> in the distance. His fists
> ball up as he sings the
> last line of "Oh
> Freedom".)

*And go home to my Lord and
be free.*

Sc.4

See, God I'm happy. She in a
better place. You needed her
more. She's watching over us.
She's at peace now. She resting
in the arms of Jesus. Ain't
gotta' worry about this old life
no more. Dancing on the streets
of gold. I promise you I'm not
mad about any of it. See!

He has made me glad, He has made me glad, I will rejoice for he has made me...

> (He hallucinates. Sounds of an explosion, people running, screaming, ambulances, and mayhem are near,overwhelming. These are flashbacks.)

Baby girl? Baby girl!

> (He digs through the rubble of the destroyed church.)

Where are you? Where are you? Hey, Daddy's here. I'm right here! Is this your hand?

> (DANIEL calls out to the passersby.)

Help me! Somebody help me! There's a hand! Moses! Joshua!

Elijah! This her right here I
think!

    (Whispers to the body.)

I got you, I've got your hand. Is
this your hand? I don't remember
a ring, did you wear rings? A
little plastic ring? Baby girl!
Answer me! Daddy's here, I'm
right—

    (He digs again, cuts
    himself, waves his hand in
    pain,but keeps digging.)

Baby girl! Baby
Girl!!

    (The memory stops, suddenly.
    The world he was seeing
    vanishes, lights sound, the
    environment is calm,
    stark,cold.)

Bridge under the water, water under the br...it was a long time ago.

Some glad morning, when this life is over, I'll fly away. When I die, hallelujah by and by... I'll fly away.

> (The song becomes raucous and unintelligible; he pulls off the invisible necktie he thinks he's wearing.)

Stomp on one. Clap on two. Stomp on three. Clap on-

> (And he stomps and dances on the snake. The African drums overtake him until he has danced himself into stillness, exhaustion, and laughter.)

Sc.5

> (DANIEL is calm.)

It wasn't a month later I could

walk by the church and not even
turn to look at it. No thoughts,
no anger, nothing. Numb is good.
You go to the dentist, or got to
get a tumor removed, or heart
surgery, anytime anyone is
invading your body, and tearing
it open, and rooting around
inside — you want to be numb.

Sc.6

I went to work that next week.
One week after the bombing I'm on
the job. Shirt buttoned and
tucked, my pants creased down the
middle — no tie. Boys at the job
say, "Rushing today? Forgot
something?"

    (DANIEL makes the tie
    motion.)

I don't say nothing, just nod,
just get to the work. Tuesday,
and someone say, "Your wife's
gotta do a better job of laying
out your clothes in the morning."

They ain't mean. There a few in
there that are pit bulls, but the
ones talking ain't that kind. I
don't say nothing though, just
nod, just try and do the work.
And the manager, he come and he
must've had nothing to do. A
whole company to run, and product
to move, and conquests to make
and he over in my little area
asking can he have a word. White
folks like having "a word." Now
those other boys ain't pit bulls,
but he is. Talks to me about
professional attire and say he
ain't want to have to warn me
again because I do good work and
he has better things to do then
to make sure I know how to dress
myself. And I nod and I don't say
nothing, just get to work. And I
nod, as I walk out the building,
and don't say nothing; and I nod
my way to the Sears, and don't
say nothing; and nod while I walk
to the men's section, and I don't
say nothing; and I stand in front
of a rack of ties, and I am a

grown man trembling in the middle
of the store. And another colored
man walk past me and he stopped
and looked. And I can't
acknowledge him because I'm not
sure if I am about to fall apart
and start crying, or if I'm about
to kill someone. I don't know me
and I sure as hell don't trust
me, not with all the nodding I
was doing. He look around for a
second and I see him decide he's
alright with dying. I see him
decide it. I know what it looks
like when a man says, "I'm okay
with leaving the earth." My
father had that look every night
he sat at the window with his
shotgun on his lap. He'd kiss my
momma, rub my head and sit and
wait and see if those pit bulls
was coming. He was always alright
with dying. That colored man in
the store decided and he say,
"You want the blue one. You want
the blue one, cause it's water,
and water the way we get back
home. And I'mma buy the blue one

and have 'em bag it and you're
gonna walk out of here with it
and be alright. And he breathed
out and slowly reached past me,
grabbed the blue one and did what
he said. And they bagged it and
he brought it over to me and he
said, now I'mma walk you home and
we gonna live another day. And
each step to my house, this
colored man say, "You got a wife
and one little girl left, you got
a wife and one little girl left.
You got a wife and one little
girl left." And we was at my door
and the colored man, he knock for
me, and my wife answer, and she
look from him to me, and she
ain't open up the screen door to
let me in. She just stand there
behind the screen and the colored
man say, "Unlock the screen
door," and she don't. "What's in
that bag?" she say, and he tell
her. And she opens the screen
door, but I don't come in. And
she takes the bag and say, "Thank
you" and the colored man leaves.

And my wife goes behind our house
and grabs a shovel and digs a
hole and stuffs the tie in it and
covers it up. And she take the
shovel in her hand, like it was a
spear, and she jabs it in the air
and starts whispering, "Not my
house. Not my house. Not my
house. Not my man. Not my one
girl I got left. Not here. You
gone from here! You gone from
here right now!" And she stomps
the little grave she made for
emphasis. Stomp on it like she do
roaches that scramble past her in
the kitchen. She went back in the
house, now I was still on the
porch, I don't know if I was
still nodding or not. But I ain't
me. And she come back with oil on
her hands. And she say, "I'mma
rub it on your neck. Okay? You
hear me in there?" And I watch my
wife decide it was okay to die.
But her hands ain't as brave as
her heart is and so they shaking
like it's winter. Like I might be
a monster. I never meant to make

her hands sha... and she prays in tongues. And usually, her praying sound like nothing, like foolishness, and religion. But there we are standing on the porch with a tie buried in our yard and my soul is slipping away and suddenly I understood every bit of holy gibberish she saying. She said, "Now you leave this 'ol heathen here with me. I ain't done with him yet. You let me keep him now, he ain't yours. You hear me devil? He mine. God done gave him to me and God himself gonna have to take him from me. But ain't no 'ol little devil gonna run in my house and take him. I'll nail your ass to the floor like Jael." Now, I don't know who Jael is, but I know my wife mean what she saying. A woman who grew up making her own sausages ain't worried about cutting nobody up. And her hands went on my neck, and I closed my eyes and saw Jesus. So now I know I'm going crazy cause I done gone

from inter-pre-tating tongues to
seeing Jesus. But it wasn't the
Jesus with the sheep over his
shoulders in a clean white dress
or eating dinner like in that
painting where they all having
bread rolls. He was sitting on a
rock in a garden, and when he
looked up, I knew he had decided
to die. He looked just like my
dad did, just like that man in
the store, and my wife on the
porch. And when I opened my eyes
— I was sitting in my arm chair,
with my wife on my lap, she must
have run outta oil, so she was
smearing me in butter. I guess it
don't matter what kinda' grease
it is. I'm sitting in my good
armchair, shirt off, shining like
a honey glazed ham, and I want to
tell her "No more butter!" but my
body isn't working. Hasn't worked
without leading for the last 5
hours. She on my lap praying and
greasing me like a baking sheet,
and she say, all quiet, "In his
precious name I pray." And my

arms woke up. I mean they worked and I could feel them work, like they'd been strapped down and suddenly they was loose, and I wrapped them around the woman who was calling me a heathen in tongues and asking God to spare me, and I held her. Held her for the first time since the bombing, and the wake, and the funeral. Held her until she screamed into my neck about her baby, about our baby, about God being mean and good and good and mean. Did that until she fell asleep. When she woke up it was around 2 in the morning. I went ahead and told her I would be losing my job over a tie today. And she said we'd make it. And that was the best thing she ever said to me. We made love right there in the chair, greasy, and I went to work a few hours later tieless, and ready. I don't know where my oldest was...hmm. I hope she was at her auntie's. They live down the block and sometimes she'd

stay the night with them...
Shoooooot, if she was home
during all that... Shooooot

(He smiles.)

Sc.7

We don't go to that church no
more. They built it back up, but
we ain't go back. My oldest
daughter only older by a few
months but she got all the
markings of being born first. She
never want us helping, always
looking down the road to what's
next. Only time she ain't that
way's on Sunday. Same thing each
time, My brothers escort us
there. One stay on the street,
one stay by the door, one come in
the sanctuary but he stand in the
back. They started doing all this
after the bombing. Couldn't
convince them otherwise. Even
though my oldest got me, her

momma, and all her uncles she
still holds my hand. I thought
she was doing it for me. 'Cause I
don't want to be in nobody's pew.
Don't want to be singing. Don't
want to be preached at. And I
tell my wife and baby girl to go
to the bathroom before we leave
cause ain't nobody going to the
bathroom there. Soon as you can't
hold it we gone; we coming home.
And they don't fight me on it.
They scared of the bathroom too.
Which means we leave church most
times during the altar call —
which be another two hours long
anyway. The only reason I'm going
is because last time I didn't, I
lost the ocean. What a man do if
he lose the ocean and dry land?
So I go, but I don't want to and
I thought that's why my oldest
had my hand. And we was maybe
three or four months into going
to this new church and we was
leaving early like we do and just
as we crossed the threshold onto
the sidewalk, I see her breathe

out. Which made me think back
through the whole service. She
had my hand the whole two hours
and as the time went on she
squeezed my hand tighter and
tighter 'til she was near
crushing me. I know cause every
Sunday my hand is throbbing for
at least an hour after service.
She crushing me 'cause she's
holding her breath like she's
underwater. And first thing I

can't figure out is how in
the world is she not breathing
for two hours! Ain't no Negro
sermon shorter than two hours.
And how come I ain't notice she
don't breathe no more? Ain't been
breathing for months. So Sunday
come again and this time I'm
ready. Before we leave I take my
oldest, and set her on the table
so she and I are about here.

> (He motions eye to
> eye.)

And I did for my eleven-year-old
the same thing I used to do for
them kids paying me to
inter-pra-tate their dreams. I
looked her in the eye and lied.
"God told me in a dream, he say,
'Tell my daughter that I have sent
three angels to her home.' And I
say, 'Thank you Lord, is that one
angel for me, one for my wife, and
one for my baby girl?' And God
say, 'No, they are all for your
daughter' and God told me to tell
you when you running out of air,
shout Hallelujah, and the air will
come rushing in." So, we walk into
that little church and sat where
we sit and my oldest daughter's
grip on my hand is starting to get
tight. And I'm watching her and
she ain't breathing and so I
pointed to the corner where ain't
nobody standing and I say, "There
one is, right there. You see him?
Big joker. Taller than me. He
frowning. He ready, the second
you give him the signal, he

ready." And she look over and she squint and she is wringing my hand to death and it's quiet because they praying over communion and she roars from the bottom of her little soul "Hallelujah!" And the room is stunned because Negros got a time and place for hollering. They like to wait for the organ to be going, and the choir to be singing, or the preaching to be high. A couple of folks ran out the building thinking that it was getting bombed. And my baby girl is roaring and ushers are making a bee line over to her because ushers got control issues. But I'm not going to let her fight for air all by herself so I stand up and she jump up on the pew so she almost tall as me and we Hallelujah-ed until my wife went into a fit of a dance. Whirled like a chocolate covered helicopter, arms for blades. Dress bouncing, head flinging, people diving out the way. And

Heaven shoved itself into that
tiny little church and sent the
whole congregation into a
beautiful hysteria. There was so
much noise my brothers all rushed
in, ready to kill every Negro in
the place. Spirit so high I saw
Joshua wipe away a tear. You hear
me? Joshua! And in the middle of
all the tambourines, and
clapping, and ecstasy, my baby
girl grabs my face and she say,
"Look daddy, I'm breathing."
Hallelujah.

Sc.8

You think when you become a daddy
you know what you're doing after
the first one. My oldest was
easy. My wife say soon as I come
in the house she'd stop her
hollering. I ain't have to pick
her up, she just know I was home
and she'd just coo and smile. The
youngest one wasn't studying her
big sister. Didn't matter if I
was home or not if she wasn't

happy the whole block knew it.
Atlantic was always trying to see
what we was up to. She ain't
never want a nap snatching her
big head this way and that trying
to see what all's going on. My
wife shouting. "You gotta hold
her head, Daniel, Lord have mercy
her head!" And I'm holding it,
she just don't want it held she
want to be free! It's three in
the morning and Atlantic go to
hollering, and I nudge the lunch
counter. I say, "Somebody want
another plate." And my wife go to
crying, like I told her her momma
passed on. So, I go with my wife.
And I sit on the floor, like this
here, and she got the baby and my
wife sittin' between my legs. And
she get the baby on her good and
I say, "Take a nap if you can, I
stay up and watch." I wasn't
through the sentence and my wife
head is drooped and I'm reaching
round her to hold the baby in
place. But the baby trying to see
me. She just nosey. So I starts

talking to her so she know what
I'm doing. I say, "Hey baby girl?
You hungry? Gone and eat now. Yo'
momma heavy leaning on me like
this. She a good mommy ain't she.
Yeah, I think we'll keep her. Oh
your big sister, she sweet she
just need a little time to get
used to you." I nudge my wife
when the baby looks done. My wife
does that thing women do to make
sure babies ain't hungry no more,
and then she passed Atlantic to
me. "Burp her." she say, and I
do.

    (DANIEL walks with the
    baby back and forth,
    patting her back gently.)

You're the star I'm following
Back to where my soul began
You're my way back home.
You're the water and the
waves In my arms I see God's
face.
You're my way back home
Back where I belong

You're my way, back
home

(The baby burps.)

Sc.9

My wife and I fought over names.
I wanted to name our baby girl
Atlantic. She want to name her
after her great grandmother. I
wasn't naming my child no
Willowmina Marie. Sound like a
woman with a face like a cast
iron skillet. What somebody want
with a burnt up, bumpy faced,
cast iron skillet? See, I'm
thinking about her future. She
was gonna be sunlight and the
sound of ocean waves breaking on
the shore, and the way back home.
And she was all of that - for 10
years she was every bit of that.
Did you know someone could steal
the ocean? I didn't either, but
they can - they did.

Sc.10

What your momma wanted to name
you, got put on the paper, but I
say, "I get to pick her
nickname." Indians look around
'em and see what nature is doing
when a child born. An eagle
flying by, you Flying Eagle. They
see an ant got a crumb on his
back and you Crummy Ant. I like
that, nature being a part of it,
having its say in our story. I
asked your teacher about that
book, gave her the money to buy
it and it came quick. Like it
knew we was goin' to see you,
goin' to name you again. Had it
under my left arm when I went
down there to identify your body.
I claimed you as mine when you
came in this world. Claimed you
as mine when you left. Did I have
the book? Could I have had the
book? How much time was it
between the bombing and the

identifying?

Couldn't come in the mail that
quick. Maybe I didn't have it,
not yet. I bought it though. I
went to your teacher and I told
her about the book and I hold out
30 dollars. I hold out the money
and she hands me the book. Yeah,
she hand me the book and say
she's so sorry. And she don't
take it, the money. I leave with
your favorite book and it didn't
cost me nothing, because it cost
me everything. And I had it, I
had it under my left arm. My
brothers walk me there. Your
momma woulda come, but- but- she
can't... So I go down there to
identify you, to give you my name
again, our names again. I'm
almost to the building and just
as I'm grabbing the door to go
inside, a blood-stained ladybug
lands on my hand. They good luck
you know. So, you are now,
Ladybug Atlantic, it's a little
long but that's fine. Better than

Crummy Ant.
Sc.11

I tinker now. Fix folks' cars,
lawn mowers, any machine. Give me
enough time I can fix it. Had a
guy waiting while I'm under his
car. He ain't know nothing 'bout
cars 'cept what color his was,
but he out there looking like
this here. Got his arms crossed
his chest watching while I'm
working and doing all that. So,
I'm on the ground working and at
one point he say, "Your people
have a very special relationship
with God, I admire that." I don't
say nothing. For one, I'm under
the entire car. Two, it wasn't a
question, it was an observation.
So wasn't nothing needing to be
said. And he goes on, now he's
yelling through the engine parts
down to me while I'm working –
man no more than thirty, maybe
thirty five. "Why is that?" he
say. He not being snide or
nothing, just "Why is that?" So,

I come from up under the car, I got oil and dirt and engine gunk all over, and I'm looking at a man who is trying to figure everything out about my people while his car get a tune up. And I say, "I tell God I love my kids," and he say, 'I love mine too.'' I say, "One of em was killed and ain't do nothing to earn it." He say, "Mine too." I say, "I would go to hell and back to save her," and he say, "I know, I did." I say, "I want to rip off the heads of the men who did it." And he says, "I know, but vengeance is mine." And I say "Okay, but don't take too long, hear?" And he say, "I won't." And then I slid back under the car and finished what I was doing. If I'dda known that woulda' shut him up I'dda witnessed to him earlier.

Sc.12

When I turned 13 my daddy say to me. There only three options a man got: To take it, to wait for it to be given, or to leave it behind. If it's a job, an opportunity, you take it. If it's a woman's love, wait for it to be given, and if it's anything that'll tie you up to where you can't function, leave it behind. You mix any of that up, you're dead. My daddy say that instead of happy birthday. And I ain't forgot it. Down here in Alabama y'all got justice made out to be a woman. A woman with a scarf over her eyes and a sword and some measuring scales. And I ain't supposed to just take what I want from a woman. I'm supposed to let her give her love when she ready. But Daddy you ain't told me what to do if Justice don't never love me.

Sc.13

Been hearing songs in my sleep,
songs I never heard no one sing
before. They not in English. Used
to be that when I woke up the
songs would stop. Now, I turn on
the faucet and the song pick
right back up from where it left
off. I run bath water, I walk
past the city water fountain,
same song, the same slop of words
that don't mean nothing to me,
but it feels like home. I don't
want to know what it mean, so I
ain't had me a bath in a few
weeks now. Won't brush my teeth,
nothing. That colored man in the
store say water's the way we get
back. And the men in my chest is
trying to go back and I don't
know where "back" is. I don't
want to know where "back" is. We
here.

I call this meeting to order!
Daddy, tell Big Daddy, Big Daddy,

tell Great Granddaddy, and Great
- Granddaddy, tell Shaka Zulu -
or whoever it is singing - we is
here now, on this plot of dirt in
Alabama, and we ain't going
nowhere but here!

> (Thunder claps. DANIEL looks
> up. Rain pours. The sounds
> of Africa mix with the
> storm. He laughs, defeated
> and accepting it. DANIEL
> spins in the rain, arms
> open, face to the sky,
> submission.)

Sc.14

Dinner was near over. So, my
wife's putting dishes in the sink
for washing, and she come around
to grab mine and I take her hand.
Not hard. And I can't look at
her. "Could you... draw me up a
bath?" And water splashes on the
table. My wife is crying, "You
feeling alright?" She done taken

her hand from mine and she's
feeling my head and touching my
neck and I say "I'm fine. Just,
would you draw me up..." And she
say, "You ain't bathed in a
month. Ain't hardly said a word
to me, to our daughter. Your body
been here but..." Then she kisses
me like I just come back from
war. I guess I should ask her to
draw me up a bath more often
because she went into a whole
Sunday service fit jumping
straight up and down with her
arms fastened to her sides
screaming "Thank ya Lawd!" over
and over. I had to stand between
her and the lamp cause she 'bout
knocked it over, along with
everything else we had in the
house. She tired herself with all
her spirit filled rope skipping
and was laid out on the floor. So,
I went ahead and drew my own bath
and let my ancestor teach me what
the words to his song mean. I was
done being stubborn. The men in my
chest needed me to go back, or to

figure something out, and I was
going to listen - no matter what.
So step one: learn the song. Every
word. And the more my ancestor
sang it, the more crowded the room
became with sound. My dad was
singing it, my grandfather was
singing it, they all knew it-
everyone knew it but me. I hearing
for the first time what it's like
for God to sing over me and I'm in
that tub screaming and thrashing
because their voices are breaking
me open, and fracturing my bones
and gutting me out until the
language sprouts out of my heart.
Small little leaves of something
new are poking through my chest.
And the more I try each word the
further its little root system
drives into my heart, digging into
the muscle of it. I'm in the tub
singing in a home language that
ain't mine. Wasn't mine until now.
Singing it like I was never stolen
out of whatever village, I'm from.
And my voice sounds young, like
I'm 12 again. About an hour later

my wife knock on the door. I
don't say nothing. She peek in,
"Room for me?" she asks. And I
don't say nothing. And she grab
the towel and soap it up and rub
my back and I take her hand and I
kiss it, and she climb in, fully
dressed. And I teach her every
single word I'd learned until she
couldn't take no more teaching.

Used to be that my wife would run
in the house quick if it started
up to raining. She ain't want
that pressed hair to draw up on
her. Now, I gotta bring her in.
The smell of rain get to her
nostrils and she run to the yard.
Waiting for the song trapped in
the clouds to fall down, for God
to sing over her again, longing
for home.

Sc.15

Never was one for visiting
somebody grave. If they gone,
then they gone, so ain't much
sense in leaving flowers and
carrying on. I'm mumbling this to
myself as I pull on my shoes.
Saying over and over again each
mile of the 9 miles it takes to
get there until I'm standing in
front of a little plaque about
this big, with flowers in my
hand. On the plaque is her name,
her dates, a scripture. I'm
staring at it and wringing the
flowers in my hands, twisting up
the stems like I'm making a
wreath or a crown and the petals
are starting to fall off the
flowers and fly around me in
swirls. Three bouquets worth of
flower petals whirling around me
until my feet went from being
flat to being on my toes to being
off the ground all together.

(Daniel spins as the winds
of the tornado gather speed
and velocity and sings Negro
Spiritual.)

Didn't my Lord deliver
Daniel, Daniel, Daniel?
Didn't my Lord deliver
Daniel, Then why not every
man?

Didn't my Lord deliver
Daniel, Daniel, Daniel?
Didn't my Lord deliver
Daniel, Then why not every
man?

Then why not... why
not...

(The winds die down, and
DANIEL has returned to the
earth and is on his hands
and knees, breathing is
difficult.)

I had seen the groundskeeper when

I came in. He had nodded, I had
nodded. We didn't speak but I
guess me being being pulled from
the earth by a flower tornado
caught his attention. He say,
"Seem like you need this more
than I do." And he hands me a
flask he had in his inside coat,
and a compass he had in his
outside pocket. I looked up to
say no thank you, I ain't much of
a drinker, but the man was gone.
So, I poured a little of whatever
was in that flask on that small
plaque with my baby's name on it
and drank the rest. Sipping on it
until the noon sky pulled off
it's work clothes for its
pajamas. Getting out the grave
yard wasn't any problem but
getting home was beginning to
feel more and more like a fight I
wasn't gonna win.

I made a wrong turn. The
whiskey...was it whisky? Too many
wrong turns. And the roads are
gravel now. Not sure when they

started being gravel. And the
woods ain't none I know, and I
know every wooded place for
miles. My legs give out and all
of me is falling to the ground,
and when I finally land, it seem
better to just stay there for a
few hours. Just a few hours. My
eyes is closing on these woods,
and on these stars, and my
breathing is slowing to a near
stop when I feel two eyes on me
that ain't mine. Shadows got a
way of crouching and hunching and
arching and I'm not sure if
anything's really there until
it's breath reach me. Just enough
moonlight to make its eyes glow
ugly. About an inch from my face
is a hunting dog. If there's one
dog, there's another, and if
there's two dogs, there's a
hunter. And I'm not sure I care
about being mauled as much as I
bout being hung naked for my wife
and daughter to see. A whistle.
The dog left ear turned
backwards. It's his whistle, the

"come here" kind of whistle a
hunter give. But the dog don't
move, and it don't bite and I'm
praying it won't bark. I moved,
just a half a inch, to see what
kind of state was I in. He show
his teeth, and crouch, and growl
like a chain saw and I know, now,
what kind of state I'm in ...and
I ain't got no more questions.
Whistle. Dog's right ear this
time. No movement from that dog,
no movement from me. And
I says to the dog, real low,
without words. "You not looking
for me, not tonight you ain't. It
will be me you coming for soon.
But it ain't me tonight." And the
dog turn his head a little,
listening at me. Listening to me
talk to him without no words out
my mouth. Then he smell the air
deep. Sniffing me, the whisky,
Edwin's sea air, my blackness,
and he sits. He sits for a
moment. Thinking, because he know
I'm right. I ain't who he after.
Not that evening. His left ear

turn around backwards again. I
ain't hear his owner's whistle,
but the dog heard something. That
animal sniff the air like it's
money and he ain't got a dime to
his name. And I see the shape of
a man thirty feet ahead jump to
running. I catch a glimpse of his
shirt, but not his body cause
it's deep brown like mine. He
move real familiar. He the one
the hounds is after and I can't
help him. No gun, no stick, no
real balance cause of the whisky.
The forest howls and pants and
chases and I stand there,
sweating. Clutching a compass,
fumbling in the other direction
before that dog change its mind
and figure a bird in the jaw is
better than two in a bush. I
don't hear them catch that Negro.
He move so familiar, but I don't
want to figure out who he is, or
who he was. Better for my sleep
if I don't know. Move so
familiar.

Sc.16

The sun making its way up now.
Just barely and my wife sitting
on the porch when I get home.
Much as guns been a part of my
life, can't say I ever seen my
wife with one in her hands aimed
at me. Rifle. She'd nodded off,
but when she hear me on the walk
she wake up quick, rifle pointed
in the air right at my head.
Cocked. A jealous woman's the
worst kind. She had said, on our
wedding day, she'd shoot me dead,
or worse, if I started taking to
watering other women's gardens. I
knew those words was the words
she'd be ready to say just before
she pulled that trigger. I say,
"Ain't nobody grass green 'cause
of me. You hear me! Only garden I
been tending live at this house
here, and she holding a shotgun!
Only garden I frolic in is right
there on my porch looking to
shoot me dead. Come smell me.

Ain't no other woman here, just
dirt, and dog, and death."

And she lower the gun, not all
the way. Just some of the way,
and she closes her eyes. Close
her eyes and walk around my soul.
Look through it the way
detectives search for clues. Walk
through it slowly with the gun
still trained on me while she
investigates. I knew when I
married her she could walk into
people's souls. Her family been
the judges of black folk
arguments long before that boat
ride here. If you lying, they
know it. My wife say, they just
good at discerning spirits,
that's how she call it "spirit
discerning." But it ain't just
that. I don't know what all it
is, but it ain't just that. Her
entire family are discerners,
marrying her was the most
dangerous thing I ever done. They
can't walk through a person's
soul without the person's

permission but I ain't have
nothing to hide. So when I
proposed her momma was ruthless,
searched deeper than she should
have shining in shadows I didn't
even know was there, opening
cellars, rifling through attics
tearing through my whole self.
That's when I heard the threads
starting to snap, the stitching
of my soul to my body was tearing
apart and my wife screaming
"Momma stop!" My mother-in-law
never gave me an apology for
almost killing me, and I never
asked for one.

My wife ain't never demanded I
let her walk through my soul
since then. In 17 years I ain't
never give her reason to ask, but
she walking through me now,
looking for signs of a woman.
When she ain't find anything she
say, "Why you out here hollerin'?
We do our talking inside like
decent folks." She say it like
she ain't have no rifle, and I

wasn't almost a headline on every colored newspaper in the South. I didn't move off the good rug until I talked her all the way through my night and saw her neck relax. Wasn't a high chance she'd shoot me on the good rug. Her momma gave her that rug. I just kept on talking 'til every one of her veins went back to where they was before she loaded that gun.

That night I go to pray to thank God that my wife ain't kill me and I don't get far into the prayer before I feel the song wrench my insides. Seem like the roots is reaching into my belly and around my guts and there is more song coming out of me then I remember learning. I sound like a child when I'm singing it though. When I'm talking to my family I sound like me- but when I'm praying and the song come up- my voice cracks, and I sound like I'm 12 again.

Sc.17

Showed my oldest the compass. She
looked at like it was magic.
Maybe it is. She run to her room
and come back a few minutes later
with a chain. She slid the chain
through the loop in the top of
the compass to make it hang like
a charm. "Where this chain come
from?" I ask. She smile, she got
a sneaky smile that come with
secrets and surprises. "Big
Daddy," she say. "One time me and
sissy went exploring in the yard,
and Sissy said in a dream Big
Daddy told her there was a
treasure underground. So, we
digged up holes and found this."
We been keeping it all this time.
I lower my head so she can put it
around my neck. It's already
turning green, and ain't worth a
cent past 5 dollars. And she
says, "I do it by myself now, but
used to be at bedtime Sissy and

I, when we say our prayers we ask
God to watch out for you and
Mommy, but we didn't say your
real names. We didn't want the
tie to find you, so we would say
your heart names. Momma's name is
Bow and your name is Arrow." And
then she kisses the top of my
head. And just as she leaves I
hear me say, "Am I a good arrow?"
And my oldest stops and looks at
me and turns her big lips to the
side thinking. "When you're aimed
at something." She say. "If your
Momma's the bow and I'm the arrow
then who doing the aiming?" I
ask. "The same one who did the
whittling I guess." She say, and
then she bound out the room and
close her door cause she done
talking.

Sc.18

In baby girl's book it say boys
who are entering manhood got a
whole process they go through to

becoming men. I'm reading the steps and I realize why I sound like a kid when I'm singing my home song. I haven't done all the steps to be called a man, not in their eyes. See first they get sent out from the tribe to face an obstacle or something. Did that. I talked that dog and my wife out of killing me. Next they learn the warrior songs. I think that's what I learnt in the bathtub. Most times they get a new name, "Arrow." They are circumcised and after that they find out what part they expected to play in the community. My oldest said I was a good arrow when I was aimed at something. But you can't skip steps. Soldiers ain't sent on mission until after boot camp. I didn't eat for three days. Couldn't eat. Ain't easy for a man to be thinking on cornbread and greens when he considering what I was considering. Wasn't nobody in my house to talk to about it and

none of the men in my chest was
offering up advice or lining up
to go first. Who you ask to
circumcise you? What friend that
good of a friend? Ain't nobody
got no friends like that. Where
you bring it up, at the church
picnic? On the third night of my
wife putting up left-overs, she
lay there next to me and I know
she about to ask about me not
eating. She done already crossed
of sick and upset. I know her
list, she always start with them
first. So, I told her. And she
went and got the Other Lands book
and read it. Went and got her
Bible and read it. Another three
days went by before she came back
with an answer. "Ain't no
instructions," she say.
"Everybody had it done and ain't
a single instruction." I thought
that meant we couldn't do it. And
I figured, for all involved, that
was probably for the best. 3 AM
that next morning I reach for my
woman and she ain't there. I

listen in the room, make myself
listen through the whole house
and I hear in the kitchen what
sound like shears snipping in the
air. White folks say they get
a "lump in their throat." Wasn't
no lump in my throat, it was a
mountain. My wife is sharpening a
small blade. I know this blade.
Her mother gave it to her as a
wedding present. Slipped it in
her hand when she thought I
wasn't looking and whispered. And
my wife said, "He ain't like
that, Momma." My wife got these
big thick lips you can read 'em
from across the street. And her
momma didn't say nothing more,
but my wife took that blade
anyway. I ain't tell her I knew
about that blade. Been making
sure it stay in the third cooking
book on the left, where she think
she been hiding it for these 17
years. She feel me in the room
with her and she say, "Where you
want to do this?" And I don't
know how to feel about my wife's

happiness. She not trying to be
happy. She trying to be solemn,
but she is looking like we about
to jump on the bus to see her
family on that cattle farm and
stay all year. "My daddy say folk
love sausage but they don't wanna
know how it's made! I ain't
sharpened knives in years seem to
me. It's been...when we get
married?" I can't hear her to
answer, my eyes is on her momma's
blade and I'm wondering if my
wife really believed I was almost
eaten, or hung, or both. And
she's talking to herself, making
sure she don't forget any steps,
because something about
circumcision and making sausages
seem about the same to her. And I
ain't know I didn't trust my wife
until we was on that bathroom
floor. Ain't trust her worth a
cent. As she prayed before she
started I'm sitting up with my
legs spread like this here, cause
I got a mind to watch to make
sure she don't get carried away.

And she prayed two things. That
God would guide her hands, and
that God would guide my flight.
And while my eyes were still
closed, thinking about an arrow
soaring in the air with big eagle
feathers tied to the tail end of
it, my wife reached behind her
and grabbed a steel pot I ain't
notice she brung with her, and
knocked me right upside my head.
When I woke up it was Thursday; I
was in my bed; and I still had
what was important to life, just
looked different. My wife is a
good woman. Dangerous, but good.

Sc.19

You ever see a man who ain't sure
where he headed next? He either
one of two things, angry and
doing nothing, or angry and
tearing up everything. But he's
angry any way you slice it. Anger
don't live in the same place on
everybody. For my momma, anger
live in her hips. Her walk would

get tight like newspaper print. I
was maybe nine or ten and my
momma tripped down the stairs. I
don't know where we was coming
from, but there was maybe seven
or eight stairs down to the
street and she flopped and
flipped down every one. Her dress
was trying to get out of the way,
so it flew up over my momma's
head to keep from getting dirty
on them stairs. So, there go my
momma, like a rubber ball bumping
and bouncing down the stairs
headed straight for the sidewalk
and into the street. I was so
stunned, I ain't go help her up.
Tell you the truth, I sat right
on the top of those stairs. Sat
down like I was on the toilet and
needed time. I couldn't believe
the size of my momma's legs. She
had legs like a Kentucky Derby
racehorse. I'm sitting on the
steps trying to figure out why my
momma's legs wasn't soft and
jiggly. Why my momma's legs look
like they could kick a hole in

the wall. I'm thinking on the stairs and my momma is screaming because her dress is in outright mutiny and she tangled in her own clothes. Seem to me the dress had a mind to come all the way off and my momma did not agree. After a minute or two, another lady had helped my mother to her feet. The two of them beat that dress into submission, put her shoes back on, picked up her pocketbook, and pulled her slip back up and over her hips. Momma had scratches all up her arms and scrapes on her face, and skinned up her knees pretty good, wounded her pride mostly. "Is that your boy there?" the lady asks my momma. If my momma had a pistol in her hands right then...

"That's him," she say. I climb down the stairs, slowly, just in case the devil get in them stairs and try and make me lose my trousers falling down to the street. We walk all the way home when usually we rides the bus.

Walk all the way there and my momma's walk is tight. Not no sweet swinging gait, like she do on Sunday. When it's Sunday, my daddy like walking behind my momma. On Sunday my momma walk like cursive, like the writing of a love letter with swirls and loops and flourishes of black ink on the pavement. Not right now though. Right now, she walking like she headed to the front lines and she not coming back. She wasn't gonna slow down, and I wasn't about to ask her to, but I'm panting and I am falling behind. We on what had to be the 5th mile, and had at least 12 more to go. And finally, I hear in my chest, above the sound of my lungs clamoring for air, I hear Big Daddy say, "Talk gentle to your momma." So, I wheeze out, "Momma, I'm sorry you hurt." And she stopped and looked at me.

And I hear Big Daddy say, he say
in my head, he say, " Tell her
she purtty." Now, I'm nine or
ten, I don't want to be telling
no girl they pretty, especially
my horse legged momma, but I
tells her. I say it with my eyes
on the ground and my toes
pointing in, and I near want to
die. And my momma come to where I
am and she takes my hand, she
ain't had my hand since I was
little, and my momma did her
Sunday walk on a Thursday. She
told knock knock jokes that was
funny, and she slowed down, for
me. Slowed down for the boy she
raised that ain't have enough
sense to help his momma up when
she tripped, got attacked by her
dress, and fell down a flight a
steps into the street. My momma
must have gone a lot of years
without hearing "I'm sorry" to
get them horse legs. When we got
home she baked cookies and gave
me three and everyone else two.
'Cept daddy, he had nearly five.

And before I gobble my cookies, I
bow my head and thank Big Daddy
cause, seem to me, he was why I
had any cookies in the first
place. My momma kept her anger in
her legs, and my daddy and
brothers kept anger in their
back. I never thought about where
mine was hiding, not until I saw
one of the four fellas that blew
up the church, standing in front
of my house.

ACT 2

SC.1
DANIEL

The men in my chest are quiet. I
would have thought they'd be
hollering, but they ain't saying
a word. Nobody's talking,
nobody's moving. If this was a
western picture, this would be
where the piana player stop
playing and the bartender stops
serving, and the card dealer
ain't dealing, and the only thing
twitching is long stem mustaches.
And I'm looking for the men who
been guiding me my whole life,
cause I ain't never killed nobody
before, and I need them to tell
me how, and ain't nobody saying a
word. And the man that shoved
dynamite in a church basement and
blew up the girl's bathroom, and
blew up 4 little girls, and blew
up near all of Alabama got his
hands shoved in his front
pockets. He don't know who I am.

I know he don't know me cause he
give me one good glance and go
back to staring at my house,
thinking. Give me another glance,
cause I ain't passed him by yet.
He looks at me a third time cause
I'm standing next to him like he
golfing and I'm carrying his
clubs. And suddenly, I know where
I keep Anger. I reach out my hand
towards him and his arm move out
of habit to shake mine. I know
he'd rather hang me by my neck
before he shake my hand, but his
arm move anyway – like it's being
controlled by a string. And our
hands touch, and our fingers
wrap, and his eyes is in mine not
knowing me, and my eyes is in his
– knowing everything about him.
His wife, his address, what he
has for breakfast; what days he
go out fishing; what time he
leave for Sunday meeting; where
he work and how long he been at
it; and the gal he see once a
month and the same one dress she
wear when he go to see her. And

I'm gripping his hand too hard,
so hard that the truths tumbling
out of his soul is starting to
sound jumbled up. And I'm
squeezing his white hand to red,
back to white, and he's using the
other hand to try and get my one
hand off, cussing. Because his
whole hand is about to burst open
and he can't stop it from
happening. And his one free hand
go into his pocket and fumbles
with a pocket knife, but he can't
get the blade out. And he don't
want to whimper. He don't want to
ask me to let him go, ask me why
I'm about to rip his whole arm
off his body. He don't want to
die noisy, not in front of no
negro. And I'm about to end him.
And a ladybug lands on my left
cheek. Used to be when the girls
was heading off to bed, the
oldest would kiss me on my right
cheek and the youngest would kiss
my left. I hated when they'd try
to both kiss me at the same time.
They heads was big, because they

momma's head is big, and they'd
knock into me and bump my head,
but they'd be the one's crying.
And I'm seeing them while I grind
this man's hand into powder; and
he is on both knees preparing to
be murdered; and my eyes are
blurring because I ain't
remembered those kisses from my
big-headed girls in a long time.
And Daddy say " You gone have ta'
choose which memory'll live on in
your soul." And the lady bug
crawls from my cheek to sit on my
nose and turns and looks at me.

      (DANIEL lets go of the man's
      hand.)

And I go and sit on my porch, and
every Colored man on that block,
come out they doors, and sit on
they porches and watch that
mangled joker walk down the road.
And ain't none of us go back
inside, we stayed on our porches
all night. Some with guns on
their laps, some with bats, me

with a ladybug on my left cheek.
All of us at our post, waiting.

Sc.2

September 13,1964 I've been
hollering at my oldest girl.
Hollering at my wife. I'm not
sure why. Ain't nothing new
happened. The sisters from 16th
Street Baptist keep coming by and
bringing pies, and cakes, and
meals and telling my wife to hang
in there. The families of the
other three little girls is
talking about having a community
meeting in honor of the
anniversary and trying to see if
we want to meet. I give myself a
nosebleed hollering. "Unless you
mean all of us is fixing to ride
over there armed and ready to
straighten this mess out with
them boys who smoking cigars and
living high on the hog and free
as birds, naw we not meeting! And
don't bring us no more plates! No
more cards, no more flowers, no

more condolences. Don't come by
this house no more. Hear!" More
nosebleeds. Then, I'm coughing up
blood. And there's blood in the
toilet. Blood is spilling from
everywhere and I can't stop it.

Sc.3

On September 15, 1964 I'm hearing
explosions loud enough to make
blood trickle from my ears,
explosions no one else in my
house is hearing. So my wife have
Elijah, Moses, and Joshua carry
me down to the Negro Hospital.
The closer we get to 16th Baptist
the more screams and dust fill
the air. There were people
running everywhere? Swore we was
walking right on top of little
brown bodies,hundreds of tiny
frames in frilly socks and buckle
shoes, with little gloves and
Sunday dresses. Swore my brothers
were stepping on Atlantic.
Stomping right on her head. It
was Three against one but that

didn't matter to me. I was set on
killing them and wasn't long
before Joshua got fed up with me
and my delirium and put me in a
choke hold till I passed out and
carried me the rest of the way.

The entire hospital was starting
to stink because I couldn't keep
nothing in. They finally send
somebody to clean up the little
crowded room they had me in. Seem
like on this particular day
wasn't no one in the room but me.
The cleaning man, he walked in.
Second the door closed behind
him, that negro looked so
relieved. I can barely
acknowledge him I'm so sick, but
I see him look relieved. And I
wonder why, cause cleaning up
people's vomit and such wouldn't
bring no relief to me. And I'm
laying on my side, and my eyes
are trying to focus, and he
starts unbuttoning his shirt fast
— like he ain't got much time.
And he fold it carefully. Then he

start undoing his pants. And it
don't matter how sick I'm
feeling, I sit myself up. I'm
wishing my brother's were there
to help but I sit up and get
ready to kill a negro who's armed
with a mop and better health -
kill him right there if I need to
because what he undoing his pants
for? But he got another pair of
pants on, same color, same make
as the ones he pulling off. He
fold them quick, and he go to the
end of the bed where my feet was
at before I sat up and he lay
them on the mattress. And my eyes
are going from blur to clear but
I'm thinking, I know this negro.
He start mopping and wiping down
the room and I'm trying to catch
his face, but my eyes are burning
from me making them work so hard
and he almost finish and leaving
out. Wringing out the mop and
fixing to leave out and I say,
"You bought me that blue tie."
And he look at me as he headed
out the door, and he say, "You

got a wife and one baby girl left." And he peer out the door to see if someone coming and darts down the hallway. I hear the mop and bucket sloshing he moving so fast. And I look at my own clothes that got everything I ever ate since birth splattered everywhere. And I peal them off and I put on the ones that man left me. And in the back pocket of the trousers-

(DANIEL pulls out a blue tie. We watch Daniel move as if to a mirror and slowly start to tie the tie. Every step closer he is to completing the knot is increasingly difficult to complete. He may restart, adjust length, stall, until there is no option but to finish.)

I have a wife and one...one baby girl left. Put it on Daniel, it make white folk feel better when

you look like them, sound like
them, makes them feel safe, make
'em think twice before they hang
you. Put it on, and get the better
job. Better job more money. More
money move out. Move from here.
Take your family up to Chicago, up
to New York, up to Canada, Ivory
Coast, Ghana, Uganda, Australia
...

It might mess around and kill
you.

    Beat

But they'll be safe.

    (The moment the tie is in
    place at his throat,
    DANIEL roars. A snake
    rattle is heard, there is
    rain, thunder, drumming,
    and defiance.)

Lights Out.

Sc. 4

>(Lights Up. DANIEL is in the
>tie doing sit ups, jumping
>jacks, push-ups, jumps an
>invisible rope like a boxer
>would. Stops occasionally to
>breath, hard, because he is
>not in the shape he needs to
>be in for the mission. There
>is water to guzzle as he
>finishes his workout.)

Robert Smith come to the house.
He don't do much talking and when
he do it's hard work for him. Got
a few children my girls age, but
that's all I know. His whole face
full of questions, ain't space
for nothing else on his face
cause questions done filled it
all up. "You expecting somebody?"
he say. He don't say it loud. He
say it like he talking through a
door and it's the password to get
inside. I don't answer him. I

look at him, let him look at me,
which for him is hard work. He
say, "I would appreciate if you
having company by, that you tell
me. I'll send my wife and family
to her mother's for a few days.
For a few weeks if need be." He
say this to me with his hands
balled up, and then relaxing,
then balled up, and then
relaxing. He don't know his hands
is upset about something. I say
to him, "I wasn't expecting them
and when they came I wasn't
ready." "You gonna be ready,
Robert, or you just gonna' hope
your wife, and your family ain't
next?" Robert stared at me a long
time, then the ground, then me,
then the sky. Then he said
something I ain't expect him to
say at all, "I don't know the
first thing about working a gun."

Sc.5

A few weeks later, I'm training
every man on my block. Joshua got
men in the kitchen doing
push-ups, and men in the parlor
doing jumping jacks. Moses
teaching how to use a stick to
decapitate a man with one blow.
Elijah ain't gotta group. Most
folks think his cornbread not
cooked in the middle. When he get
to talking about summoning birds
to make his breakfast and
directing lightning... I tell the
fellas to just look interested,
he'll quiet down after a while.
Truth is though- he ain't crazy.
I seen him call ravens, eagles,
hawks, wild pigeons he ain't
never met before. They'll sit on
his shoulder like he a park
statue. Problem is Elijah talk
inside out. And when you talk
inside out folks think your mind
gone. It's safer for him that
way, if word got out he can

really do everything he talking-
if white folks ever found out. I
mean birds bringing you fish for
breakfast is one thing, calling
down fire is a whole nother story
entirely. He'd be dead in no
time. I tell the fellas to just
let him talk it out, ain't no use
trying shut him up. And so they
listen politely the way you do
someone you figure's slow and
harmless.

When it's my turn to talk I break
them into groups. I say, "We in a
hole and we need to get out. The
ladder to freedom got three
rungs. Body, mind, spirit. We get
our body strong, so if it come
down to a fight, we ain't whooped
on the first blow. We get our
mind strong. I mean reading and
understanding what they telling
us, not just schooling. I mean we
know legal talk so good nothing
get by us. And the last rung,
spirit." One of the deacons, he
speak up on "spirit." He say, "I

wonder if God don't like it this way. We ain't slaves. Ain't we content with that?" The other men looked at me, some for permission to kill him, and some for hope. I say, "If Noah ain't build that arc he'da died with the rest of them. God wasn't gonna build that man no boat and he wasn't gonna turn him into no fish. God gave him warning and ability and left the rest to Noah. Now if you don't want to build then fine. I hope you can swim."

Sc.6

Atlantic, I think I know what I was made for. I help men figure out how to survive being tied. And it's working. Colored folks doing for colored folks, Feeding ourselves, teaching ourselves, loving ourselves, you seeing all of this baby girl? This Arrow's found his target. I'm sorry I didn't know before you left here.

I would have been a different
kind of daddy.

Sc.7

I wear the tie everywhere: wear
it when I'm fixing machines; wear
it when I'm in town, when I'm on
the porch, wear it when I'm
training. Everywhere. The other
men do too. I wear it until I'm
not sure if it can come off, like
my skin has grown around it, and
into it, and ain't no getting
free from it. Some nights I feel
it trying to take my mind, like
I'm an extension of it, instead
of the other way around. Those
are bad nights. Those are busted
lips, scratched up neck, almost
dying kind of nights.

Sc.8

We meeting. House full of folk
and we trying to see how to get
more food over to the Negros in
the next town over. We doing

numbers, and figuring out where
to set up the food, and planning
and one fella interrupts.
Johnston. I know him. Been
knowing him, don't like him,
don't dislike him. He just
Johnston. Johnston say, "When we
fixing to do something?" The
other men keep talking because
they WAS doing something 'til he
interrupt. I almost don't mind
him either until he say, "We
gonna go get 'em or what?" Then I
mind him. Every man in there got
at least two white men they
wouldn't mind putting in the
ground. I got four. So ain't
nobody jumped out they seat to
tell him he was out of line. The
real Daniel, he had
inter-Pre-tated dreams but he'd
also have visions. I ain't never
had me no dreams until 19 and 63
the year I lost the ocean, and I
ain't never had me no vision
until 19 and 64, at that meeting,
listening at Johnston. The room
is still talking food pantry and

such, but I'm not in there no
more. I'm in a different room,
it's all black and I see
Johnston. He don't see me. He got
a tie draped around his neck and
it ain't tied. Then two hands,
just hands now, two hands come
floating in and tie it for him.
Johnston skin is blue black. The
hands is cream colored, like
milk. Then I'm back in the
parlor, like I never left. I say,
"I ain't never seen that kind of
knot before, could you show me
how you do that?" Johnston look
confused, then he touches his own
tie. "Ain't nothing special," he
say. He don't get up, he don't
move, his jaw gets a little
tight. So I undo my tie and hand
it to him, a few fellas watching
now, most of the others still
working though. Johnston hold it
like it's a dead rat he pulled
from up under his porch. "I was
just messing around with the tie
and it come out this way. I can't
remember how it go." He hand my

tie back to me. "Who in your ear Johnston?" I whisper it, when he was close. When he was handing the tie back, I whisper it and his body go stiff. "What you trying to say?" He say through his teeth. He talking like I'm challenging him to a fight and I'm not, but if he swing at me, he dead. And my wife smell tension from her bedroom, she a blood hound when it come to tension, and suddenly, she out in the kitchen warming up pie that was supposed to be for me and she getting plates, and making a racket, and slicing it thin so everyone get a sliver and Johnston ain't answer my question and he's going to.

Johnston look at me, look at me a long time "They know you heading this up." He smiles. "It's been a pleasure." He say as he leaves out. I wait for bullets to rain on the house, grenades, bricks through the window. But there was nothing. And the room looks at me, and I see my oldest with her arms wrapped around her mother's waist, and wife breathing shallow, quick, like the clock is running out of time. And she's right. It is.

Sc.9

We go do the community garden together as a family. We usually leave out the house round 6 AM so we got plenty of time to set up and such. My oldest look like a truck hit her. Sick as can be, so my wife say she'll stay. And I don't feel right about it, but I don't know why. Not like it make sense for her to go and I stay. Don't make sense for both of us to stay. None of that makes sense, but I don't feel right. My wife sitting on the edge of the bed watching, not scared, just concerned – the way she always is when the kids are sick. And my oldest wants to go with me, but she can't. So to make her feel better I say to her I say, "Everybody got their name but you. Your momma's Bow, I'm Arrow, your sister's Atlantic, and today you get your name." And my oldest smiles and focuses and tries to fight off whatever got her under the weather so that she can be present for her naming. I take out the compass. "It wasn't never meant for me" I say. I'm not sure if I'm lying or not, but I said it, so it's true now. "Your name is Sailor, for you will be at home on the land and on the sea- never bound, always free." I put it around her neck and kissed her head, like she'd done me, and she showed her momma like her momma ain't seen it before. And of course my wife say, "I see!" and "I like your new name" and "You not doing chores today, but when this fever breaks, you better hop to it or it'll be man overboard." And my oldest says, "So Sissy is Atlantic the ocean and I'm Sailor, with a compass to guide the way and you and momma are bow and arrow so then that makes us a battleship because it has weapons!" And my wife tells her not to over work her brain and pretends to fan her before she pops, And I kiss the people I

love, my one woman and my one
girl who together make up my dry
ground, and I leave... without the
compass.

Sc. 10

My momma named all us boys Bible
names, and so did her sister. My
Aunt, Sarah, named all her kids
Bible names too, but she like the
letter S, so all they names start
with S. I hate when folks do this.
Ain't but so many names in the
world with the same letter.

So, my cousins is called Saul,
Samson, and Shulamite and all of
them foolish, hot-headed, and wild
as weeds. Of the three, Samson got
the most sense, unless it involves
a woman. I'm talking with the
Branson family. Getting them
signed up for services, tutoring,
food, and house repairs, we'd just
added that to what we can offer -
small stuff like roof patching and
such. I'm getting them set and
here come Samson. He come in and
the woman I was talking to, she
just go to giggling. And I ain't
have to turn around to see who put

a giggling spirit on her like
that. "What you need Sam?" I say,
without looking at him. I know
it's him because Mr. Branson swole
up to five times his size trying
to get his wife back in order
after she got filled with the
spirit. Samson don't say nothing,
which ain't him. He like putting
on a show. I stop writing and look
at my cousin cause he ain't said
nothing yet, and what I see kick a
hole in my throat big as Samson's
foot. My cousin is covered in
sweat, breathing hard, he'd run
all the way here, but he can't
get out what he came to tell me.
So I say, "Just take me there."
And Sam nod's, truckin' like a
missile. Like a bullet. And I
shout to my brothers and they fall
in. None of 'em worried about
dying early, no chirren, no wives
to protect, and no fear. The five
of us in our church shoes and
button up shirts, and ties
flapping behind us. Every time my
foot hit the ground, I'm feeling
lighting all through my body.
Stomp on one, clap on two. I
thought we was headed for my
house, but two miles out we dive

into some trees. Sammy, give us a
signal, point, and say "5 miles"
with his mouth, but no voice. We
spread out. There's a plume of
smoke rising and a strange scent
in the air. I spot a stick. Pick
it up. A stick against guns. It's
sharp though. A spear against
guns. We close to the noise where
people are whispering, shuffling,
and it's colored folk. Not a lot
of them. They're circled around
something on the ground. A few
feet beyond them the land is
smoldering where the fire was. I
dropped the stick I'd picked up.
Moses had his cane ready, holding
like a bat; he much better with
stick fighting than me. Josh had
him a knife, probably had it in
his pocket; Elijah had him a hawk
on his his arm, and my fool cousin
got something look like a dog jaw
bone. What the hell was he gonna
do with that? And who dog he tore
up on the way? The circle noticed
us and parted and there
on the ground was my "dry land."
My wife and my oldest girl. I
check 'em for broken bones and
bleeding but they look fine. Look
nearly angelic- like how my

brother Moses looks when he been
talking with God. Their chocolate
skin glowing bronze like metal
just taken from out the fire. I
wrap around them. They wrap around
me. They almost too warm for me to
hold but I hold 'em. My brothers
make a circle, turn outwards,
guarding. One of the Negros that
was there when we came, he take my
cousin Sammy by the hand because
Sammy was born with a face that
looks like he in charge. That
Negro say,

"If I hadn't seen it with my own
eyes. I'm walking in the woods and
I hears they trucks and hide. I
know these trees, see, so I know
how to hide in 'em. They take that
lady and that girl there, do what
they want to 'em, and then build a
fire. I can't stop 'em, six of
them. One of me, back ain't good
no more. Only one of me. And when
they was done doing what they
wanted they thrown that woman and
that little girl in the fire. And
the fire shot up taller than
anything I ever seen. And I'm
expecting the screaming and such,
but the girl and the woman they

just stand there in the fire. And
few seconds later one them boys
say, 'Ain't we just throw two gals
in there?' And the other one say,
'Yup.' And he say, 'Then who that
third little gal in there?' And
sho nuf, there was three: a
smaller girl, the bigger one, and
the woman. And they holding hands
and fire all over them, and they
not burning. One of them boys shot
a few bullets into the fire and
nothing. Nothing. Them girls ain't
hurt. All six of 'em gone after
they seen that. Then the smallest
girl looked up in the sky and
disappeared and took the fire with
her... 'I think I'm ready to die
now,' the man said, 'Can't nothing
top that... One more thing, there
was a negro with them. I thought
maybe he was next to be hung or
something, but he ain't seem to be
worried about nothing. He ain't
watch though, turned his back on
all the carrying on them boys did.
I would have turned my back too,
but I was trying to know who the
womens were so I could tell they
people. Watching hurts. That negro
had nice shoes. Blue snakeskin,

real nice. Funny what you notice
when the world coming apart."

Sc. 11

Johnston ain't run. I figured he
might, but he ain't. He come home
and I'm sitting in his chair, in
the dark, waiting. He don't jump
into no apology. Just put down the
liquor he had in his hands on a
little table near the door and
closes the door. Turn on the
lights. Sits in the chair opposite
of me. Reach for the bottle, takes
a drink. "They was just supposed
to tear up the house, and scare
y'all," he say after about 5
minutes. "You were supposed to
take your family and be serving
the good colored people of Alabama
from 6:45 AM until 3:00 PM," he
say. He say it aggravated, like I
had messed up his breakfast
order at the local diner. I look
at his shoes. They're nice. Snake
skin, blue snake skin. "Why were
they at home?" He asks me. "My
daughter was sick." I say. He
nods. Chuckles. Drinks. There's
something going around. A bug." He
says. "How much they pay you?" I

ask. "Not enough," he says. "Those
boys had a lot more fun than they
thought they would with your women
being home." He doesn't drink
anymore. He isn't a lush, just
thirsty; and he ain't worried
about nothing, not those white
men, not me in his house, not
nothing. "Now for your women's
sake, 'specially your little girl,
I wish what happened to 'em ain't
happen. But they ain't suffer
nothing every woman in my family
ain't suffered since back past my
great grandmother. And since it
seem like your women is witches
and fire can't destroy 'em, they
be fine after a while. My sister
got hit up twice, and had two
babies that way, and she fine. You
want some water?" He say. And he
stand to fix me a glass, so I
stand. "When your sister got hit
up, was it cause you led the wolf
into the sheep pen?" I ask.
Johnston looked at me. For the
first time, he really looked.
"Course not," he say. "But what
kind of shepherd leaves his sheep
all alone?" There was so much heat
in my hands when I grabbed
Johnston's throat, it melted like

butter. Eyes big, veins ruptured. Head popped like a cork shoved in a Champagne bottle, and it rolled around the floor. Dead. I went to his momma's, she wasn't but a few steps down the road and told her her son had passed on. She sucked her teeth and breathed in all the air in Alabama. Stared at me long enough to know I was why he'd passed. "I'll send some men to take care of things in the morning. And I'm very sorry for your loss," I say. "He ended better than I thought he would," she say. Then she and she go back to snapping peas.

Sc. 12

I expected my wife to be standing on our porch when I get home, one hand on her hip, her body propped up by the post. I was almost right. She was inside the house looking out the screen door with one hand on her hip. I don't try to open it. I know it's locked. She stare at me through the black mesh screen. She say, "I still forget sometimes and make two sandwiches. I be in the middle of

cutting the second one in half
before I remember ain't but one
baby to feed. Seem like throwing
the other sandwich away hurt more
than the funeral...You took
somebody's baby away from they
momma?" I don't shift my feet- I
don't look away I just tell her
what it is because it is what it
is.

"I've been a fool waiting for
Justice to love me. She wasn't
never gonna love me."

And my wife unlocks the screen
door and moves back just enough
for me to get one foot good into
the house and she whispers in my
ear, one hand on my neck. I tell
myself don't turn and kiss her
Daniel, don't make any sudden
moves.

"You want to know how I knew you
killed Johnston?" she say. I don't
want to know, but this ain't the
time to be honest. She say, "His
soul is sitting in the corner of
our living room."

I glanced over where she pointed and didn't seen nothing.

"I tried to make him leave but he got rights here. Rights to this house, rights to us, cause of you. Justice ain't no woman you can take and have your way with whenever you get ready. Justice is the hand of God. And since you out there doing God's job for him, finish it up!" And she shove the anointing oil she stole from the church into my chest and went back to cooking. I walked all through the house, slowly, and didn't see not hide nor hair of Johnston, but I dabbed the walls with the oil, just in case.

Sc. 13

Count is up to 10. Ten men I need to find. I'm up late, planning, thinking. My wife know what I'm planning. I ain't tell her what I'm planning, she just know. She don't say don't and she don't say do. She don't hardly say nothing anymore. My house is quiet now. And I hate it. When I brought my girls home from that fire they was alright on the outside, but the body ain't the whole person.

My daughter sleeps in our room on her momma's side of the bed now. I gotta say my name as I walk up to the house, gotta make sure my oldest hears me coming so she don't burst into tears. She scared of church bathrooms, our house, and men's voices - even mine. She asks me if I locked the doors, middle of the day could be in the middle of playing and look up and ask about the doors. And when she think I'm reading and not paying any mind, she tiptoes past me to check the locks herself. Do you know how hard I worked for this house? How hard I'm still working, and the only people who matter are scared to be inside.

My wife ask me to sleep near the door, in my good chair. So I can deal with whoever might be coming in the house. She say it would make our oldest feel better, but her eyes don't look in mine and I know there's two people in my house who scared of me and so I sleep in my good chair. My wife

don't touch my arm when she passes
by. Just above my elbow, right
here, that's were her hand used
ta' go, been going there since day
one. And I'm not angry at her
about it, I ain't yelling at her
talking 'bout "Where my arm touch
go?" cause that sound crazy but I
want to shout "Where my arm touch
go! I ain't do nothing wrong!"

It don't matter if it's the worst
winter you've ever known, if you
got your good coat on you're all
right. Well this is the worst
winter in years and I can't find
my coat, and I'm not sure I ever
will.

Sc.14

My wife , sneak out of our room
one night after our oldest girl is
knocked out. I'm in my good chair,
not sleep, and she whispers in my
ear, "Get us out of here." She
don't touch me when she say it.
And I say, "Where we going?
Chicago? New York?" It's dark in
the living room, I can see my wife
form but not her face. I sit up.
I'm hoping that she'll let me hold

her. I'm hoping she'll keep talking. She talks to our daughter, asks her about school, helps her with her studying, says prayers with her at night, but not to me, not directly to me, won't look at me at all, hasn't looked at me since the fire. And I'm starting to wonder if she thought everything that happened was my fault; Like I let those boys in the house. But she here asking me to get them out and so maybe, we gonna be okay. And I moved too quickly. I was sitting up in the chair. And I must have moved too quickly. She jumped back. Grabbed her little robe closed that had fallen open and walked back to our room and shut the door.

I sat there waiting for her to come back. She didn't. Then the men in my chest whispered. "Give her room to work it out for herself. She need room. Not you. Room, and a way to work it out." And I talk with them and pray all night about what to do for my wife.

My wife don't like flowers, chocolate, nothing normal. She's a butcher's daughter. Hogs, cows, chickens, deer, pigeon, quail, you name it, she's fed it, cleaned it, killed it, and served it on a plate. So that next morning I go down to Odell's farms and buy me a hog about 29 weeks old, at least that what Odell said it was. And I get a rope and walk the thing to my house on the leash. When I was close to the house I shout for my oldest who come to the porch. "Gone and tell your momma I got something for her. She rush inside and moments later my wife come to the door, apron on, with her veins popping out the side of her head, until she see my gift. I used to doubt how smart folks would say pigs are but that pig was fine the whole way to my house. Ain't give me no trouble. The second it saw my wife in the screen door it had a fit. I didn't hand my wife the rope. Oh no, I told my wife, "He's yours, I expect patties for breakfast." Then I bent down and untied the pig right there on the walk. I freed it. So it set off to running down the street. Like hot

grease sizzling in a skillet my
wife runs into the kitchen, grabs
a knife, throws off her apron,
jumps out her house shoes and
shoots down the street like her
head was on fire. She and that pig
ran for blocks, leaping over
hedges, trampling rose bushes,
scrapping, and falling. My wife
with a butcher's knife in one hand
and them both screaming and
squealing for miles. When she came
back she had the thing over her
shoulders. Its slit neck draining
all over her dress and congealing
in her hair and down her front
side. The blade in her teeth as
she walked. I couldn't watch her.
She was in the yard screaming and
stabbing the pig and weeping and I
couldn't watch. She took the knife
and made a circle around her and
the pig and shouted at God about
him having better make this right
or she'd fix it herself. The
neighbors had a time. Curtains
parted and little brown faces
smushed against window panes all
down the block. She split the pig
in two and chopped off its head
and had it hanging on the
clothesline like it was dirty

drawers. She would come in the house every now and again cause she forgot something she needed, praying quietly, the whole time. At one point I was at the sink getting water and she wanted to get by and she touched my arm as she passed. She ain't notice it, ain't turned to smile at me, or nothing, but I stared at my arm now smeared with pig blood in the shape of her fingertips and I breathed out for the first time since the fire.

We had sausages, links, pork chops, bacon, for nearly three weeks. Coming toward the end of that three weeks, my wife say good morning to me, and she looked at me when she said it. I must of looked crazy because our oldest say after a while "Y'all alright?" And my wife goes back to her plate and keeps eating but I don't have another bite, I don't need it, I don't ever need to eat again.

Sc. 15

My girls should both be sleep in
bed. And I hear walking, small
feet. I turn my plans over. The
plans say Moses got two houses
and Joshua taking care of 2
houses, Elijah getting the last
two houses. I tell my brothers to
leave the men who took baby girl
to me. I got them myself. I'm
planning what I'mma do when my
oldest daughter walk in staring at
the paper I just turned over. I
watch her gather courage, so I sit
very still so it don't flutter
away like it has been doing these
last few weeks. And she say, "When
it's morning time, the compass
point North when it's by you. But
at night time, the compass spin
around and around. See Daddy?" I
look at the compass and it ain't
spinning. "See how it's going?"
she say. I don't see nothing. The
compass just pointing one way like
it always do. But she look
worried, and I learned my women,
so I say what I always say when I
have no idea what they talking
about. I say, "I see," and she
smile just like her momma. "So

Daddy, whatever you thinking at night time, it's making you get lost." And I say, "Daddy's just trying to figure out how to make things right." And she says, "I'm the sailor right?" I nod. "Okay, you're off course, this proves it." And she shows me the compass again, and it still ain't moving much at all, but for her it's moving like a bicycle wheel. "Thank you Sailor," I say. And for her sake, I take the papers I'd turned over, and tear them in two. "Cross your heart" she say. And I breathe deep and cross my heart and my chest burns like I set an iron on it. The biggest grin you ever saw spread over my child's face, and she reaches for my face. I bend toward her and she kisses my head. Then she skips away to her room. Now she ain't gone in her room at night since the fire. She leaves the door open and I hear her talking in her room like she used to before the church was bombed. She say, "You see Atlantic, everything's gonna be just fine. We almost home."

I waited a few minutes before I
pulled my shirt back to look at my
chest, sure enough there were two
bright red-ish purple welts where
I drew the cross.

Newspapers had a fit about them
campfire boys who tried killing my
family.

    (Reads newspaper)

Birmingham's Police overwhelmed
with six unnamed homicides and no
leads. Six men of fraternity, but
otherwise no relation, all met
grisly deaths yesterday evening.
Two of them were found burned to
death.

    (to himself)

That was Elijah.

    (He reads again.)

Two were found drowned in their
respective bathrooms.

    (to himself)

Mo.

(He reads.)

The last two men had limbs
gruesomely severed by what police
are calling an unusual serrated
weapon.

(to himself)

Josh.

(DANIEL continues to read.)

Police are searching for leads on
the cases. If you have any
information…

(He puts down the newspaper,
chuckles.)

Sc. 16

I wish I knew how the real Daniel
died. Doesn't say. Moses' temper
keep him in the wilderness till he
just dry up. Elijah ride up to
heaven on a chariot. Joshua - old
age, I think. But, I keep
checking. Ever since I tore up the
plans, I hear rattling in the
house. Snake rattles. I don't tell

my wife or my oldest because they starting to be more like how they used to be. Starting to heal up a little bit. My oldest went digging in the yard again and found her some more jewelry that Big daddy had hid. This time, it ain't junk. This time, it's so real I start sweating. My wife leap all the way up to the ceiling. And my girls hug each other and laugh and say, "Look baby." And I'm breathing because they gonna be just fine. I ain't ask my daddy where he got that from, or Big Daddy, or nobody. I just breathe deep cause my family's gonna be okay without me. And while they dreaming of new dresses and finishing school, I'm listening for the dogs. They gonna be coming. I ain't follow the rules right, I was supposed to kill those men who took Ladybug Atlantic. And I didn't follow the rules, guess I ain't never been the kind to. I put Sailor to bed that night with her compass; I tell my wife she pretty and I'm sorry (so she don't develop no horse legs) and I wait in the parlor.

(There is a scratching sound at the door, like an animal trying to get in. DANIEL whips open the door.)

And there on my porch is the colored man from the store, and from the hospital. And he say, "I think you've met my friends," and them dogs from the forest start coming down the walk. He was the negro I thought them dogs was chasing. He say, "You letting them boys get away with it? Come on Daniel. Change your mind and I'm gone for another 65 years. You got a wife and one little girl left."

(DANIEL considers then shakes his head no.)

And a ladybug lands on my left cheek, and she and I walk with the colored man down the road and into the moonlight.

Sc.17

We was at a creek and the whole way there I'm waiting for the dogs to jump me, or the ground to break open and snatch me down. We get to

that creek and he stops just a
step away from the water. He say,
"You leaving this way? Your
brothers took care of them men who
tried to destroy your wife and
oldest girl and you won't take
care of the men who stole your
baby girl from you? Your brothers
more man then you are, more
husband to your wife than you is.
You been the runt your whole
life," he say. "You try to make up
for it by acting smart, but what
your woman want is a protector,
not a calculator. She want someone
who handles business. Them boys
with the dynamite won't get a slap
on the hand for another 39 years.
That's what happens when you leave
vengeance to Jesus, he wait for
them boys to live their best lives
and then when they old and gray
maybe he take him to the woodshed.
Most times though- he don't. That
fine with you?" And I feel my
hands start to warm up the way
they did at Johnston's, and at the
church bombing, and at the
campfire.

"Show your wife she married a
lion. She need someone who she can

respect. You leave this earth
without killing those men, she'll
spit every time someone speak your
name. Show them white boys you a
man. I'll bring 'em to you. Hand
'em to you. Last chance, Daniel."
And as long as I been sitting in
someone's church, I know what
crossing the river mean. It mean
no going back. And maybe I
wouldn't be worried about it if my
momma hadda' named me Lazarus, but
she didn't.
"Sir, what happens to Johnston's
soul?"
"He'll follow the men in your
house for as long as he's got
rights." And I breath out because
ain't no men in my house for him
to follow. The welts on my chest
feel fresh, stinging like salt and
alcohol was being rubbed into 'em
at the same time.

I say, "I made a promise to a
little sailor that I'd stay on
course, Sir, and that's what I'm
going to do."

And with that I close my eyes to
see my wife again, her with the
shovel for a spear, her in the

kitchen, her in the bathtub, her
in my arms. I see her and my
oldest getting freed and delivered
on the pews of that little church,
and my baby girl with that book. I
don't fight the snakes I feel
wrapping around my wrists and
coiling around my ankles. I don't
fight the wind rushing to my face
as I fall towards the river or try
an' keep the water from swimming
into my lungs because I'm staying
the course, and this is how the
course ends. Now my brothers, in
order of being most dangerous, is
Joshua first, then Moses, then
Elijah, then me. I told both my
daughters this, every day when
they was old enough to understand.
If they was in trouble and they
momma and me wasn't around, they
should ask Uncle Elijah, first,
then they Uncle Mo, and then if
Moses and Elijah is completely
dead or crazy, then they ask they
Uncle Josh. Ask Uncle Joshua last;
I say it with my face looking like
this here because I want them to
know asking him at all means
asking for trouble. I'm almost
done with dying, and I hear them.
There's more river inside my body

than outside, and more snake venom in me than blood, but I hear them. The three most hazardous negros I have ever known. Joshua snatch me up like I'm a catfish on a line. Elijah always got on this stupid fur coat he got from an old priest. He call it a mantle, but it's just a old ratty fur coat. He wrap it around me and now I look like a dead rabbit, and I hear Moses winding up. I taught my brothers how to revive people. Chest compressions, use your lips to put air in the lungs, then do the chest compression. They didn't like it. It works. I show 'em don't know how many times and they still ain't like it. Would rather let you die then put air in your lungs themselves. I'm almost all the way dead and I know being revived by my brothers is about to be the most painful thing I've ever experienced. Moses's walking cane is twirling so fast it's sounding like a windmill then a turbine, then a propeller. I couldn't open my eyes, but I don't need to, he been my brother my whole life and I know what he's doing. Joshua is holding my corpse

body up in the air above his head.
Elijah's arms is stretched out
like he directing a choir and
lightning is striking - lightning
always strikes when Elijah gets
riled up. And Mo got that stick
spinning like them I-Talian boys
when they tossing pizza dough up
in the air. And when he got the
stick going at top speed, I hear
Moses run at me, and then I don't
hear no running because he is
flying in the air. Whack! That
stick goes right cross my chest,
and then Elijah shock me with a
lightning bolt at the same time,
and me and Joshua who holding me
up, we fry like breakfast potatoes
in a skillet. And I want to say
while each bone in my chest is
breaking and my body is being
electrocuted, All you Negros had
to do was put some air in my mouth
and chest compressions!

        (DANIEL coughs and spits up
        water revived, pained, but
        revived.)

Joshua throw me over his shoulders
like he a fireman and Elijah say,
"You bleeding all over my mantle."

Like I want to be wrapped in his
crazy fur coat in the first place.
But he ain't taking it off me
because it's warm and I'm
shivering and can't make myself
stop shivering. Mo make his staff
turn back into a cane and he walk
like an old man again, faking. And
when we get up to the house, I
know my wife is on the porch
because I hear Joshua say, "Uh
oh."
"Where was he?" She say.

  I'm listening for the gun. Joshua
puts me down slowly, and wraps my
arm around his neck because I
can't stand up, not yet. I try to
lift my head enough to see if she
got a gun, but she not on the
porch. Took me two minutes to
realize that one eye is swollen
shut because she been standing to
my left and I didn't know it until
she touched my face. "Where you
been Arrow?" she asks me. This the
first time she call me Arrow, and
when she do, it make me feel like
I can run all the way to hell and
back without breaking a sweat. I
say, "Just gettin' baptized." And
I feel Joshua trying to disappear

because he don't like sweet talk.
He'd rather be asking the sun to
stand still so he can kill a
couple more fellas then endure
sweet talk. But he can't go
nowhere 'cause he holding me up
and Elijah fur coat is holding me
together, and I'm barely alive and
they all know it. "You sent them
for me?" I ask. My wife nods. "How
you know where to send them?" She
say, "We tied together, ain't we?
That's how." And she looks away
and starlight flickers in her
eyes, and I'm not sure why she's
crying. "I Ain't sure whose baby
I'm holding." she say, "Not sure
if you'd want it, or me, if it
come out with blue eyes." And
Joshua's grip on my arm gets
tighter because the ground under
me went soft. And now I know why
she ain't rush me into the house.
She ain't sure if I'mma want to
stay. And I say, "Everything you
ever touched, end up good, this
won't be no different." And my
woman is kissing every bruise
away, and Joshua clear his throat
because he about to blush to death
on my front walk. And my brothers
laugh and Moses carry me inside

because Joshua is sick of me and we all sit in my living room. My brothers rotating watch duty on the porch, my wife tending to me with alcohol and rags and fussing, my daughter with her compass and my house warmer than it's ever been.

Sc. 18

She having a boy. She say she having a girl cause she carrying it low, or carrying it high. I can't remember which is which. I don't care if she carrying it side to side, I know it's a boy, saw it in a dream. So I'm already talking to him. I say, "Ay, boy." And I wait for him to look at me, and when I think he looking at me I tell him all kinds of things. But tonight was different.

> (DANIEL looking at his wife's belly, maybe rubbing it at first).

"You not ever gonna fit," I say to the boy in her belly. My wife's eyes got this big a'round. "I had a dream last night you was worried about fitting and you was getting in a whole mess of trouble trying to fit. So, we might as well get it out now, you ain't never gonna fit, but you will belong. See a car got on it a steering wheel, only one, and four tires. The tires is friends because they just alike, you understand? They working hard outside, you working hard inside. You won't fit in with them, but you belong to the car just as much as they do and you can't forget that. You'll always belong." And when I was done her whole belly leaned toward me, not my wife, the boy in the belly. And I just rubbed her stomach, right where he was pressing, and told him all night, "You belong here." And after a while, Sailor started saying it to him, and my wife sang it, and I stopped having those dreams about him being worried and getting in a whole mess of trouble. Instead, I started having dreams that he had dreams- just like I do.

Sc. 19

It's 1 in the morning and I'm
awake because my wife is
uncomfortable and seeing as she as
big as a barn every time she move,
I feel like the whole bed about to
flip over. And I'm trying not to
get mad at this big ol' bear in my
bed. And I hear her go to holler.
Wasn't hard cause she turned her
face to mine to make sure I knew
she was hollering. She ask me to
catch the baby because he coming
too fast to get the midwife, and
I'm thinking, tell him to slow
down. And she say, "He crowning?"
And I look when I don't want to
and I see his head is busted in
half and I don't want to tell her,
but she know something wrong. My
wife scream "Sailor" and our
oldest come crashing into the room
still holding her binky that she
swear she don't sleep with anymore
and she say, "Momma the butt is
coming out first." And I am
relieved to death that his head
ain't split in two and my wife say
to me, Reach in and turn him
around. So I tell myself, this
just a machine. Just fix the

machine, but when I go to fix it
the machine start hollering and
the cogs and wheels is warm and
angry and I feel like I'm trying
to stuff a turkey I ain't have
sense to kill first and about an
hour later, I was holding a
steering wheel. My wife say, "Mr.
Midwife you catch 'em, you clean
'em, you name 'em." And I ain't
say nothing because I'm not sure
if what I want to name him is the
right thing. And my wife say,
"Daniel, name the boy you
raising." And I whisper it to his
momma because I don't want to say
it out loud if it ain't right.
"That's a hard life you wishing on
him," she say.

"But he'll become second in
command over the nation." I say,
"If he survives prison." she says.
"He'll survive it momma." Sailor
whispers. My wife breathes
deeply. "Okay - my wife says,
gone head, he waiting." And my
oldest daughter is holding my
wife's hand, and the moonlight is
shoving through the window trying
to see, and I take him close to me
and stand up because it seem like

I should be standing and I say:
"On behalf of Bow, that's your
momma, Ladybug Atlantic and Sailor
- your sisters, and myself, we'd
like to say we so glad could join
us, Joseph."

And my wife say, write it down
for him Daniel, how he got here,
just in case we not here to tell
him. And I told her I would and I
did, that what this is. I'm sorry
about Johnston, but I'mma do
everything I can to figure out how
to get him gone. And I probably
won't say it much to you at all,
uhm, I love you steering wheel.

  (There is a baby crying, this
  is JOSEPH. DANIEL picks him
  up, rocks him, and sings.)

Ain't no pit that can keep you
Ain't no prison can hold you
They can say all sort of things
against you
But you'll win time and again.
Cause you're mine
I'll be fighting beside you.
Cause you're mine
And I'll be there to guide you
'Cause you're mine

Because you're mine

>   (The baby coos, Daniel rocks
>   him, hums. The sound of rain
>   pours and the sounds of
>   Africa mix in with the
>   Downpour. Daniel wraps the
>   baby in a blanket and takes
>   him outside and dances and
>   laughs with the baby. Just as
>   DANIEL is heading back
>   inside and the lights dim the
>   sound of a snake's rattle is
>   heard, DANIEL hears it, turns
>   and roars.)

Black Out.

'Cause You're Mine
Lullaby

Crystal Rae

Way Back Home

Crystal Rae

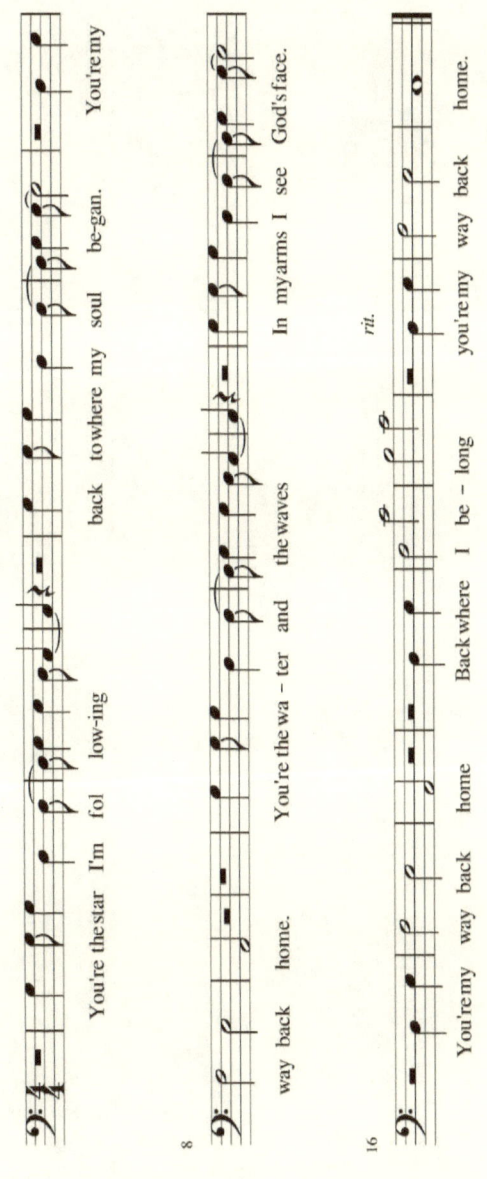